Chapter 1

No Time for Pretending

Annie came down the garden path and opened the front gate. In the field on the other side of the street, Penelope Potter's pony, Pebbles, was dozing in the sun. Yesterday, just before Pebbles was about to eat it, Annie had found a four-leaf clover in his field. Jamie said the clover was incredibly lucky and had tried to buy it, but that's brothers for you. Now it was taped on the wall above her bed, four round leaves and a stalk. And although its greenness was fading, Annie hoped its luck would grow and bring her what she always dreamed of: a pony of her own.

There was no sign of Penelope, and Annie wondered if she had time for some pretending. She would climb the gate, stroke Pebbles's soft nose, and imagine he was hers.

Magic Pony

A Dream Come True

For Jo, with love and thanks

No part of this publication may be reproduced, stored in a retrieval system, or transmitted in any form or by any means, electronic, mechanical, photocopying, recording, or otherwise, without written permission of the publisher. For information regarding permission, write to Scholastic Ltd., Euston House, 24 Eversholt Street, London NW1 1DB, United Kingdom.

ISBN 978-0-545-21320-2

All rights reserved. Published by Scholastic Inc., 557 Broadway, New York, NY 10012, by arrangement with Scholastic Ltd. SCHOLASTIC, APPLE PAPERBACKS, and associated logos are trademarks and/or registered trademarks of Scholastic Inc.

12 11 10 9 8 7 6 5 4 3   10 11 12 13 14 15/0

Printed in the U.S.A.   40
This edition first printing, May 2010

Magic Pony

A Dream Come True

Elizabeth Lindsay
Illustrated by John Eastwood

SCHOLASTIC INC.

New York Toronto London Auckland
Sydney Mexico City New Delhi Hong Kong

"Hurry up, Jamie," Mom shouted from the front door. "We'll miss the bus." She spied Annie by the gate. "I can't imagine what he's doing."

Annie sighed a big sigh. The pretending would have to wait.

Jamie bounded out the front door, slamming it behind him, and was at the gate in three leaps.

"Don't hang around," he said, giving Annie a push. "What're you waiting for?"

Jamie was jingling, his pockets full of birthday money, and Mom was taking him to the magic shop in town to spend it. Annie had to tag along, too, so she was bringing her money just in case.

Jamie was going to be a magician when he grew up, a fact he told everyone. He'd even made a flowing black cloak to prove it. Annie was going to be a famous horse rider, but she didn't know how yet. Mom and Dad couldn't even afford riding lessons, so owning her own pony was an impossibility. *Would finding a four-leaf clover make any difference?* she wondered. Mom put an arm around her shoulders and gave her a squeeze.

"Cheer up, Annie."

Annie managed a smile just as Penelope Potter rode past on her gleaming new bicycle.

"Not going horseback-riding today, Penelope?" Mom asked.

"I am later," Penelope said. "When I've finished riding my bike."

A new bike and *a pony*, thought Annie. *It's people like Penelope who have all the luck.* And she trailed after her mom and brother to the bus stop.

It was market day in town and they had to weave their way between the busy stalls to Cosby's Magic Emporium, Jamie's favorite shop. It was tucked down

a little side street off the market square. The storefront was faded and the paint was peeling. By the time Mom and Annie arrived, Jamie had disappeared inside. Annie peered through the dingy window and was about to follow Mom in, when something at the back of the display caught her eye.

"Coming, Annie?" Mom asked.

"Can I look a minute?"

"If you want. I'll see what Jamie's up to."

Tucked behind the card tricks, eyeglasses with funny noses, itching powder, pretend blood, wizard hats, and magic rope was a poster. A chestnut pony

with a white star and blaze, wearing a mischievous expression, looked Annie straight in the eye. Annie couldn't imagine what a pony poster was doing among all the jokes and magic tricks, but it made no difference. She wanted that poster. She knew the exact place she would pin it on her bedroom wall. With a little laugh, she hurried into the shop to ask how much it cost.

Chapter 2

The Poster

The shop bell tinkled and Annie closed the door behind her. She stepped around two large cardboard boxes to where she could see Mom and Jamie watching an old man with gold-rimmed glasses and wispy gray hair demonstrate a magic trick.

"Hocus-pocus, rim tin tiddle," he said,

then triumphantly held up what looked like an ordinary piece of rope.

Jamie gasped in admiration.

"That's awesome! I saw you cut it up. I know I did." He took the offered rope and looked at it carefully. "I'll definitely take that trick."

The old man's eyes twinkled behind his glasses.

"Thought you'd like that one."

"Annie, come and say hello to Mr. Cosby." Mom waved at her to come forward.

"Interested in magic tricks are you, young lady?" the old man asked.

"Sort of," said Annie, not wanting to offend him. "But I like ponies best. How much is the pony poster in the window, please?" Annie reached into her pocket for her purse.

"That pony needs a good home," said

Mr. Cosby, coming out from behind the counter. He shuffled past the cardboard boxes and opened what looked like a cupboard. When Mr. Cosby took out the poster, Annie realized it was the door to the window display. "Four dollars."

"Four dollars!" Annie felt her hopes fade. She knew she didn't have four dollars.

Mom sighed. "Annie, are you sure you want another pony poster? It's a lot of money."

"Yes, I do. It's the most perfect picture. And if it was on my wall I could pretend it was my pony. We could pretend together." She blushed. She didn't like talking about her pretending. It was a secret. She hurried to count out her money.

Mr. Cosby closed the door to the cupboard that wasn't a cupboard and looked at the poster with satisfaction.

"This is the only one there is. There's not another like it." He walked back toward the counter and Annie was sure he whispered, "So you're very lucky to get it."

"Lucky?" said Annie. "Oh, yes, I am. The pony's so beautiful. I couldn't bear not to have him."

"Well, how much money have you got?" Mom asked.

"Three dollars and twenty-seven cents," Annie replied, making a pile on the counter.

Jamie, who had been trying to work out the rope trick, suddenly took an interest.

"I've never seen horse posters here before."

"Don't usually get them," agreed Mr.

Cosby. "This is a one-time-only special just waiting for your sister."

"So how did you know we were coming?"

Mr. Cosby smiled in a vague sort of way and, realizing he was not going to get a reply, Jamie went back to his rope trick.

"Mom, please can you lend me seventy-three cents?" Annie asked.

"Are you sure, Annie? It's all your allowance spent at once."

"Very sure," said Annie, who would have paid even more if necessary.

"He's named Ned," said Mr. Cosby. "I think you'll find him a good value for your money. In fact, I know you will." Annie put her three dollars and twenty-seven cents in Mr. Cosby's hand, and Mom added seventy-three cents more. Smiling up at Mr. Cosby, Annie was sure he gave her a wink before rolling Ned into a tube and slipping on a rubber band.

"You look after him," he said, handing Ned over. "Find him a nice place on your wall and he'll look after you. He's all yours now."

"Thank you, I will. Really I will."

Mr. Cosby nodded and smiled as if he knew Annie would.

On the bus ride back, Jamie was impatient to get home, eager to try out his new tricks. Annie hugged her poster,

thinking of wonderful new games to play with Ned. She couldn't wait to take another look at him. When the bus pulled up to their stop, Annie and Jamie jumped down to the sidewalk, leaving Mom to follow more slowly.

"If you're going to run on ahead," she said to Jamie, "take the key." And she handed it over.

Annie didn't run but did trotting steps, pretending to be on Ned's back.

When she got to the field gate, Penelope cantered past on Pebbles, turning him to jump a line of blue barrels. Annie would have stayed to watch, but the poster seemed to wriggle in her hand and remind her it was there. She didn't wait for Pebbles to jump the barrels again. She ran up the path to the front door and hurried in after Jamie. There was something important she had to do.

Chapter 3

The Pile on the Landing

Annie's feet clattered up the stairs and along the landing to her bedroom. It was the smallest room in the house — other than the bathroom — and a bed, a chest of drawers, bookshelves, and a desk were all that could fit inside. Her hanging-up clothes went in the big wardrobe in Mom and Dad's bedroom. Sometimes, she minded that Jamie's room was twice the size of hers, but he was the oldest and that was that. But she liked the view from her window, which included the whole of Pebbles's field, and from her bed she was close enough to see Esmerelda, Prince, and Percy, her three china ponies on the windowsill, as well as all her pony pictures on the wall.

Annie slipped off the rubber band and unrolled her new poster. Ned looked up at her from the bedspread while she reached for her pushpins, hardly taking her eyes off Ned's chestnut face. Somehow he seemed bigger, more head and shoulders than she remembered him in Mr. Cosby's shop. There, she was sure, she had seen his back and the top of his tail. Now he was like a pony looking out over his stable door. Puzzled, she thought she must have remembered wrong. But it didn't stop her from wanting his head to pop out of the picture. Of course, it didn't — which was sad.

She pinned Ned up above the chest of drawers, the best place for her to see him without getting a cramp in her neck. Then she flung herself onto her bed to try

it out and glimpsed the four-leaf clover, still taped to the wall above her head.

"You did bring me luck," she told it. "You brought me Ned." She lay back and gave the chestnut pony a good long look.

Slowly she closed her eyes and began a new game of pretending. She told herself a story in her head and it went like this:

Me and Penelope Potter are best friends. Not true in real life, but never mind! I get a halter from Penelope's tack room and Penelope is there.

Penelope says, "Hello, Annie. Want to go riding together?"

I say, "Yes, that would be nice. I was just on my way to the field to bring Ned in."

Penelope says, "I'll come with you and get Pebbles."

Together we walk to the field gate and call.

"Ned!"

"Pebbles!"

The two ponies come trotting over, one a pretty chestnut with a long flowing mane, one white stocking, and a white star and blaze on his face. . . .

Annie opened her eyes just to check on the star and blaze. Yes, Ned was looking straight at her. She had gotten it right. The white stocking she had made up, not being able to see his feet. She closed her eyes again.

The other pony is a pretty dappled gray. In no time at all we fasten on the halters and lead our ponies to their stables. I enjoy doing this because I am able to feed Ned juicy pieces of carrot and he nuzzles my pocket for more.

Annie sighed. What would they do next? Oh, yes, grooming.

*I am carefully bolting Ned's stable door
when a voice calls me —*

"Annie! Annie, come down at once.
It's dinnertime. I'm not telling you again."
It was Mom's angry voice getting in the
way and not the nice pretend voice
she had given Penelope. Annie shut her
eyes tight but otherwise didn't move.
She wanted to brush Ned's ginger coat
and make it gleam. This was her first real
pretend with him and she didn't want to
stop.

"Annie!" Jamie banged on her door.

"What?"

"It's dinnertime. Mom says you've got to come downstairs now."

"I will."

"And if you don't, I've got to make you."

"Go away, horrible boy. I'm coming." Annie sat up with a groan. It wasn't fair.

Why did dinner have to get in the way? The pretending was going so well. On the other hand, she was feeling pretty hungry. She swung her legs to the floor. Ned's eyes seemed to follow her to the door, which she liked.

"See you later," she whispered.

Downstairs in the dining room, the table had already been set. That was her and Jamie's job, and she guessed Mom must have been calling for ages, gotten fed up, and done it herself. Dad wasn't back yet, but Annie knew he would be soon. No wonder Mom was mad.

A key turned in the front door lock and the door slammed. It was Dad, and he came in looking really fed up.

"It's been one of those days," he said, slumping into a chair just as Mom came out from the kitchen.

"As bad as that, dear?" she said, dropping a kiss on his forehead. "I'll make you a nice cup of tea. Food'll be on the table in a couple of minutes."

They were just getting to the best part of their meal, dessert, when there was a startling crash, bang, and *gerflumph* from upstairs. Annie froze, cake halfway to her mouth, and listened. If she hadn't known it was impossible, she would have thought a large animal was clomping above their heads — an animal like a cow or a horse. A horse!

She dropped the cake and made a dash for the door before anyone else even moved. Upstairs in her bedroom, she found her bedspread crumpled and all the books from the bottom shelf knocked onto it. And something else was wrong, too. It took her a moment or two to figure out what it was. Ned had disappeared. The poster was still there but, apart from a mass of blue sky, it was empty. She stared, astonished, until the rest of the family pounding up the stairs sent her running. The door to Mom and Dad's room was open and she peeped around it. Their bedspread was horribly crumpled, too, although nothing else seemed different.

Then Annie noticed the funny smell. Everyone arrived at the place it came from at the same time. Annie could hardly believe her eyes: Outside Jamie's room was a large pile of dung.

"Good grief," said Dad. "Horse muck!"

Mom put her hands to her face.

"All over the carpet!" she wailed.

There was a moment's stunned silence, broken by something clumping in Jamie's room. Annie put her head around the door. A real live chestnut pony with one white stocking pawed at the carpet and swished his tail. Annie gasped, eyes as round as pools. It was Ned!

"How did you get out of the picture?"

"I fell out. A mistake. I meant to jump." And he could talk!

Dad pushed the door open, and in a flash Ned was gone. Annie couldn't figure out where, until she saw a tiny pony trot along the windowsill and hide behind the curtain.

Her brain worked fast. She saw that Jamie's black cloak had been stepped on and was ripped. Between that and the dung on the landing, no one was going to be pleased that there was a pony loose in the house, especially one that went from big to small and seemed to come out of a poster.

"Is this some kind of a joke, Annie?" Dad asked.

"No," said Annie. "No." She couldn't think of how to explain the smelly pile on the landing. "But dung is very good for roses."

Mom was stone-faced.

"I don't know how that mess got here, but I want it cleaned up at once, Annie. Do you understand?" For some reason everyone was blaming her.

"Yes," said Annie. "I'll do it right away." No one knew it was Annie's poster pony, and she didn't want them to find out if she could possibly help it. Because this, she realized, was a dream come true, and she just wanted everyone to go away so she could find out more about it.

Chapter 4

The Fight on the Carpet

Annie hurried to the garden. She took the shovel from the toolshed and the bucket from the greenhouse. Mom, Dad, and Jamie had gone back to finish their dessert — which, under the circumstances, Annie found surprising. She knew she wasn't the one who had dumped horse dung on the landing and couldn't imagine why they all thought she was. In the end she decided it was lucky that they did, even though she had been told to go to her room after cleaning up and was definitely in trouble.

She shoveled the smelly pile into the bucket and carried it downstairs and out through the back door. Unsure where to put it, she took it to the bottom of the garden and dumped it on the compost heap. She washed the shovel and rinsed the bucket and put them back where she'd found them.

Back on the landing, she sniffed the carpet and squirted it with carpet cleaner. She scrubbed hard and, by the time she'd finished, the messed-up patch was as good as new and much cleaner than the rest of the carpet.

She sneaked into her bedroom to

check Ned's poster. Still empty! Then, remembering the rip in Jamie's black cloak and Mom and Dad's crumpled bedspread, she hurried to tidy things up. Her own room could wait until later.

It only took a moment to straighten the bedspread, but the ripped cloak would take some time to mend. Thank goodness she practiced sewing with Mrs. Plumley from next door, so she knew what to do. She didn't have much time. Soon Jamie would finish dinner and almost certainly come upstairs to practice his magic tricks. She tiptoed across to the windowsill, expecting to find the miniature Ned behind the curtain. But he wasn't there. No time to look for him now.

She hurried into Mom and Dad's room in search of some black thread, pins, and a needle. She found the sewing box in the big closet. As quickly as she could, Annie pinned together the torn sides of the cloak and began to sew.

She was not quick enough. She was only halfway down the rip when there was an angry cry from Jamie's bedroom. Now that he'd discovered his cloak was missing, what was she going to do? Own up to it, she supposed.

"What do you mean you ripped it?"

"I didn't exactly say I ripped it. I said it got ripped. It was an accident and I am sewing it up."

"You'd better. You wouldn't like it if I ripped something of yours, like that silly pony poster." Jamie stomped out of Mom and Dad's bedroom. Annie went after him, grabbing him by the arm and pulling to stop him from going into her room. She knew if he was angry he could do anything.

"Please!" She wailed. "Please. I am

mending it. I'm really sorry your cloak got ripped." She clung on, almost pulling off Jamie's sweatshirt while he kicked her bedroom door. *Bang, bang, bang!* She would not let him get to her poster. It would ruin everything. Jamie tried his hardest to shake her off. Then he took a deep breath and from his red and furious face came a loud yell.

"GET OFF!"

But Annie had no intention of getting off. She had gotten a grip and wasn't letting go. It took all her strength, every bit, and she just hoped that someone, Mom or Dad, would arrive before Jamie finally won, because he was bigger and stronger and would win in the end. She gritted her teeth as Jamie pulled her across the carpet and pushed at her bedroom door. It started to open.

From out of the corner of her eye she saw something small and chestnut, with a flowing mane and tail, canter through the crack into her bedroom. There was a

shrill whinny and the door banged shut, pushing Jamie back so hard that he knocked her into a crumpled heap. Before Annie could get up, Jamie shoved all his weight against the door. Annie thought he had won. But the door wouldn't budge.

To save face, Jamie jutted his chin forward and leaned toward her.

"If my cloak isn't mended properly, now, this instant, I'll get that poster and rip it into a million pieces — see if I don't!"

"I am mending your cloak. You know I am and I'll finish it now. I promise."

"You'd better." At last Jamie's temper was cooling and, feeling safer now that her bedroom door was stuck, Annie hurried to finish the sewing.

"If you two don't knock it off, I'm coming up there, and you'll wish I hadn't!" Dad shouted up the stairs.

But, because they had already knocked it off, Annie hoped he wouldn't bother. She went back into Mom and Dad's room and sat on the bed, feeling shaky. She and Jamie didn't often have fights, but when they did, it was always upsetting.

Annie picked up the cloak and found the needle. She sewed with her best tiny stitches to hide the rip as much as possible, although she knew the cloak would never be what it used to be. If only ponies didn't have such hard hooves. As soon as she thought of ponies her mind began to spin. How could a pony come out of a picture, grow to its proper size, and in the blink of an eye shrink to almost nothing? How could it speak? It was almost too much to take in. And as Annie's fingers sewed, another question popped into her head.

How would she get back into her bedroom?

Chapter 5

The Pony Under the Bed

The cloak was finished at last, and when Annie held it up the mend was hardly visible. Mrs. Plumley would have been proud of her, and even Jamie was impressed when she gave it back, although he tried not to show it.

"Mmm, not bad," he said, putting it on with a flourish that turned the cloak into giant bat wings. "Want to see a trick?"

"Not just now," said Annie. "I've got things to do."

"Like unjamming your bedroom door?"

"Oh, it's not jammed now," said Annie, crossing her fingers and hoping she was right. "Something got wedged under it."

She hurried out of Jamie's room before he decided to come and look. Outside her door she put her ear to the wood and listened. The room sounded empty, so she turned the handle. The door glided open as it usually did, and she cautiously went inside.

Ned's pony poster was still a blank and there was nothing on the bed except the books knocked from the shelf. She quickly put them back. She searched on

her windowsill, where Esmerelda, Prince, and Percy stood in an undisturbed line, still looking across the front garden to Pebbles's field. There was nothing on the chest of drawers, so where was he?

"Ned," she whispered. "Ned, where are you?" She got down on her hands and knees. Under the chest of drawers there was nothing but dust. She turned to the bed, lifting the blankets so she could get a good look underneath. "Ned, are you there?"

On the far side of the gloomy space she saw him trot in a circle and shake his head, then stop to paw the carpet before

cantering toward her. He was the same size as Percy, the smallest of her china ponies. It was like having Percy come to life.

Annie kept very still, her eyes gleaming as if she couldn't quite believe what she was seeing. When Ned reached her knee, he jumped up and landed on her thigh. Before Annie realized what she was doing, she stroked his tiny back. There was a sharp blast of air and she was suddenly squashed against the bed, with Ned towering above her, the size of Pebbles, tacked up and ready with a saddle and bridle. It was astonishing!

"Get on," he said. "Quickly, before someone comes in."

Annie didn't need to be told twice. She climbed onto the bed, grabbed a handful of mane, and put a foot in the stirrup. The moment she was on his back, a great wind blew. She shut her eyes against it.

When she opened them again, she was clinging on like crazy and Ned was cantering across a stretch of brown hills. He turned sharply around a large square tree and she nearly fell off. It took her a moment or two to realize that it wasn't a square tree after all, but her bed leg, and that now she, too, had become tiny. She was wearing a riding hat and put a hand up to its silky smooth velvet. Not only that, but she also had on jodhpur boots, jacket, shirt, and tie.

"I'm wearing riding things," she said, astonished, and couldn't imagine where her ordinary clothes had gone.

"Of course," said Ned. "Anyone ever teach you to ride?"

"Not really," said Annie. "When Penelope lets me, I take a slow ride on Pebbles. I have trotted twice but I've never really ridden."

"Since I'm your magic pony, I will teach you. That's what I'm here for."

"Yes, please," said Annie.

"Then take hold of the reins." Annie picked them up with one hand and held onto the mane with the other. Being small, she realized, meant it would be easy to learn to ride in her bedroom — there was lots of space. But Ned had other ideas and trotted out to the landing. At the top of the stairs Annie gasped. The drop looked huge.

"By the way," Ned said. "Tell your brother to keep his hands off my picture."

"Oh, he was angry about his magician's cloak, that's all," said Annie. "Now that I've mended it, I'm sure he won't think of that again."

"It was lucky I managed to wedge the door shut in time. If that picture gets ripped, that's the end of me."

"Oh, no!" said Annie.

"Oh, yes! So not a word to anyone about where I come from."

"Not a word. I promise." Annie clung on while Ned pawed at the carpet.

"Hold tight and off we go."

It was a shock when he jumped down to the first stair. Annie had barely recovered her balance when he jumped to the next. She knew there were fourteen stairs and clung on grimly. To her amazement, she was still on his back when Ned jumped to the hall floor. He trotted toward the living room, not seeming to mind Annie bouncing around like a sack of potatoes. Stretching high above them was the door, solid and thick, but open just enough for them to get through.

Mom and Dad were watching the
news on TV, two giants sitting in
mountainous chairs in front of a
flickering screen. Spread across the
carpet were feet so big that Annie
couldn't see to the other side. They were
joined to trousered legs that reached up
forever, or so it seemed.

"Feel like a canter across the carpet?" said Ned, setting off. Knowing she was no bigger than a mouse, Annie felt afraid. And no sooner had she thought *mouse* than she thought *cat*.

"Tabitha!" From the kitchen came the *bang bang* of the cat flap. "Stop," said Annie. "There's Tabitha . . . !"

Before she could properly warn him, Ned took off, galloping across the carpet toward Dad's big feet. Instead of going around them, Ned jumped the feet in a

great bound, landing with a thud that left Annie halfway up his neck. The pony didn't stop but turned and raced to the kitchen, sliding to a standstill on the tiles. In the middle of the floor, paw raised (for until that moment she had been washing it), sat Tabitha.

"I've been trying to tell you!" panted Annie, just barely clinging on. "We've got a cat!"

Chapter 6

Cat Scare

Two green eyes gleamed and a fluffy tail twitched. Ned reared up and his front legs thrashed. Annie fell, the terrible wind a roar in her ears, and landed, to her astonishment, in the sink, her normal size again. Wedged between the dirty dishes in the dishpan with her legs up in the air, she struggled to pull herself out. There wasn't much room: Ned filled the kitchen. His tail swished, knocking knives and forks from the draining board and spice jars from the rack. He snorted at Tabitha and ignored the chaos of jars and silverware smashing and crashing at his feet.

The shock of it all turned Tabitha into a cat brush. Her coat stuck out in every direction. But not for long.

Dad burst into the kitchen. "What on earth's going on?"

Ned vanished and Annie felt for the telltale riding hat. That was gone, too, and her ordinary clothes were back.

"For goodness' sake, Annie! Get out of the sink!"

"I can't." Annie scanned the floor for signs of Ned. So did Tabitha, who was beginning to get the hang of this creature that went from small to big and back again. She and Annie caught sight of Ned at the same time, as he cantered behind the vegetable rack and hid at the back of the garbage can. Tabitha pounced and batted behind the can with her paw.

It was a relief to Annie to find Dad's strong arms at her shoulders, lifting her from the sink to the floor. She wriggled past Dad and grabbed Tabitha.

"Stop it, you," she said, and unceremoniously dumped the struggling cat in the living room and shut the door.

Dad looked grimly at the mess of knives, forks, and broken jars that covered the floor.

"What is going on?"

"It was an accident," Annie said, feeling her wet bottom. "I'll clean it up."

"You'd better believe you will," said Dad. "With the dustpan and broom. Be careful not to cut yourself on the glass."

"I'll get the dustpan." Before darting to the cupboard where the dustpan was kept, Annie opened the back door. She wanted Ned to escape to the garden and find a safer hiding place than behind the trash can.

The moment Annie began to sweep, Mom opened the kitchen door.

"Oh, what a mess!" she exclaimed. And not being a cat to miss an opportunity, Tabitha raced for the garbage can. Annie dropped the dustpan and dived. The garbage can went flying and through the hail of empty pizza boxes, wrappers, and cartons, a tiny pony bolted for the garden. Tabitha scrambled from between Annie's arms and took off after him.

"Leave that cat alone," scolded Dad, stopping Annie in her tracks. "You're just making everything worse."

"The kitchen's a pigsty," said Mom. "Annie, how could you?" Annie didn't even try to explain. With one eye on the back door, she propped up the garbage can and swept as fast as she could.

Finally, the kitchen was clean again, and Annie hurried to put the dustpan away. There was no sign of Ned or Tabitha.

"Can I go now?" she asked.

"Yes," said Mom. "Straight up to bed. And get those wet jeans off."

"But —"

"You heard what I said."

Annie knew there was no arguing, so after a quick look out the back door she hurried through the living room and upstairs. Only instead of going to her bedroom, she went to the bathroom, where she closed and locked the door.

The bathroom window opened up above the kitchen roof. Annie had never actually climbed out from here before, but Jamie had. Jamie had reached the ground that way. If he could do it, so could she.

Annie put down the toilet lid and climbed onto it. Then, with one foot in the sink, she balanced her other knee on the windowsill and opened the window.

From there she scanned the garden for signs of Ned and Tabitha. Laundry hung limp on the line and the shed door was open. She would have to be careful. The twitch of a tabby cat tail drew her eye to the canopy of rhubarb leaves billowing out from the vegetable patch. Tabitha, it seemed, was underneath.

Annie pulled herself up and perched in the open window. Turning, she eased herself down, hooking her arms over the sill until her toes touched the tiles of the kitchen roof. She had made it.

Crouching low, she decided the best way to the ground was by the old trellis nailed to the wall at the far end. She crawled along the tiles and carefully let herself down.

Hoping she could not be seen from the living room, she hurried down the path, ducked under the clothesline, and crouched to peer under the rhubarb. It was a dark, dense, stalk-filled forest. Ned, if he was there, could be hiding anywhere. Tabitha's green eyes glinted.

"You leave Ned alone, Tabby," she warned. "He's a pony, not a mouse." Tabitha blinked but her tail twitched just the same. "Ned, are you there?"

There was a thump and a clump and a bang.

"I'm here." The voice didn't come from under the rhubarb, it came from the shed, where Ned's head peeped out, proper pony size, just as if he was looking out from a stable.

"What are you doing in there?" Annie asked.

"Hiding, of course. What do you think?"

Annie ran to the shed and put her arms around Ned's neck. She was so happy he was safe! Then she noticed the saddle and bridle were gone. She looked around for them. On the floor lay Dad's claw hammer and wooden mallet.

"Sorry, I knocked the tools off with my tail," said Ned. Annie picked them up and put them on the workbench.

"But where's the saddle and bridle?"

"They come and go when I don't need them," said Ned. "Just like your riding things."

"So it's real magic then," said Annie, eyes wide.

"Hat, boots, jacket, saddle, bridle, it's all real magic, including me!" Ned gave her an affectionate push with his nose. "And now that you've found me, you can help me get back to my poster. That's enough excitement for one day. Ready to carry me?"

"But, I can't!"

"Yes, you can." And in the blink of an eye, Ned was his tiny self, trotting across the floor.

Annie scooped him up in cupped hands and, with a quick look to check no one was watching, hurried to the trellis. She balanced Ned on her shoulder and slowly climbed, one foot after the other, arms pulling, until they reached the roof, where Ned jumped, landing neatly in the gutter. He trotted along the black trough, leaping over the leaves and twigs that had collected there.

Annie crawled beside him across the tiles. She was beginning to think they would make it without further mishap when she looked up and saw Tabitha crouched on the windowsill. Ned scrambled from the gutter and Tabitha flew at him, claws unsheathed. In an instant Ned was big again, balancing dangerously on the slippery tiles. With a terrific effort he leaned back on his hocks and jumped for the bathroom window.

Annie put her hands over her ears, expecting to hear the crash and splinter of breaking glass, but there was only silence, broken by Tabitha scuttling from the roof, her confidence shaken. Quickly, Annie put her hands over the windowsill and hauled herself up. She tumbled into the bathroom in time to see the tiny Ned cantering across the bath mat. She managed to close the window before an angry banging started at the door.

"Hurry up, Annie. You've been ages. What are you doing in there?" It was Jamie, fed up with waiting.

"Coming," said Annie, undoing the lock. But before she had a chance to pick Ned up, the door was pushed open and Jamie barged in.

"You're not the only one who wants to get ready for bed." Ned shied sideways and galloped for the landing.

"Sorry," said Annie and rushed after him.

"You should be." And the bathroom door slammed without Jamie noticing a thing.

Inside her room, Annie closed the door and ducked down to look for Ned under the bed. He wasn't there. Neither was he on the windowsill or under the chest of drawers. It was only when she sat on her bed that she saw he was back in the poster. She sighed a huge sigh of relief.

But a pony poster cannot talk, and as Annie pulled off her wet jeans and pulled on her dry pajama bottoms, she began to miss him.

"Ned? Did you really happen?" she asked, running a finger across the poster's shiny surface. It was cool and only paper, not a bit like the warm, silky fur she longed to feel.

She sat back on the bed and stared up at him.

"We had an adventure, didn't we?" she said at last. "A scary one." But already she wasn't quite sure. It could have been her imagination, except she'd never have thought up anything so exciting.

Mom came in to kiss her good night.

"Night-night, love," she said, stroking Annie's hair. "Lost in a dream as usual."

"Not really." Annie smiled. "At least, I don't think so."

"Well if you aren't, you soon will be. Have sweet ones," said Mom. "See you in the morning."

It was after Mom closed the door that Annie noticed a long chestnut hair on her bedspread. She picked it up and her heart beat fast with excitement. It must have come from Ned's tail!

"It is true," she said. "You did happen." Annie looped the hair carefully over her four-leaf clover so that it hung above her on the wall. Then she snuggled down.

Maybe, just maybe, Ned would come to life again soon. And with that wish on her lips and her fingers crossed to make it come true, she fell fast asleep.

Magic Pony

Join Annie and Ned on their next adventure!

Annie was in the kitchen, opening a sardine can so she could give Tabitha her special Saturday pussycat breakfast. This morning, the toaster had refused to work and, before staggering outside with a pile of laundry to hang up, Mom had explained that you can leave a toaster to work on its own, but bread under a broiler needs watching. On the broiler pan, four slices of well-browned toast were reaching a point way beyond done. The sardine smell had Tabitha winding herself eagerly around Annie's legs and purring loudly, and the smell of burning toast had Annie diving to the rescue.

There was a knock at the front door.

"Somebody's at the door!" Dad shouted from the living room as he unscrewed another tiny part from the broken toaster. In her panic to save the toast Annie didn't hear — she was too busy switching off the broiler and blowing on the burned pieces.

"*Meow*," said Tabitha as a reminder.

"Coming."

Annie put down the broiler pan, grabbed a fork, and dug out the sardines. Tabitha stretched up and, shoving her nose into the bowl as soon as she could, dived in.

There was another, louder knock.

"Somebody please answer the door," shouted Dad. Jamie's footsteps clattered down the stairs and clumped across the hall. "Thank goodness someone's going." Another screw joined the collection on a plate.

"I burned the toast."

"I know. I can smell it." The hall door opened and Jamie came in. "Who is it?" Dad asked.

"Mr. Potter! He didn't stop. He asked me to give this letter to Annie." Jamie held out a pink envelope.

"What letter?" asked Annie, darting to look.

In typical brotherly fashion, Jamie sent the letter spinning across the room. Too curious to complain, Annie caught it.

"I know what's in it and I told Mr. Potter you would," said Jamie.

Annie looked at the envelope. Her name was printed in bold black letters and underlined. "Penelope typed it on her new computer."

"Well, aren't you going to open it?"

"I am," said Annie, skipping across the room. "Upstairs."

"What about the toast?" cried Dad.

"Jamie can do it."

"That's not fair," objected Jamie. But he was too late. Annie was gone.

Once in her bedroom, Annie pushed the door closed and sat on her bed. Then she looked up at the pony poster above her chest of drawers. The head of a handsome chestnut pony stared down at her.

"Ned," said Annie. "This is a letter from Penelope Potter. Why do you think she's writing to me?" Annie waited, hoping for a reply, but none came. The pony in the poster remained a picture. "Please magic, please work today," wished Annie. "Make Ned come alive." Annie jumped from the bed. Her three china ponies, Esmerelda, Prince, and Percy, were looking out of the window. She looked out, too. But this morning the field across the lane was empty. Annie tore open the envelope and pulled out a pink sheet of paper.

"It's even got a pony logo," she said. "I'll read it to you. Then maybe you'll come alive. We could have an amazing magic pony adventure all day if you did." She looked longingly up at Ned, remembering her first glimpse of him in the window of Cosby's Magic Emporium, the shop where Jamie bought his magic tricks. Had Mr. Cosby known all along

Dear Annie,

I was sick in the night and now I feel yucky. Today I was going to a horse show, but Mommy says I have to rest. Pebbles is in his stable. He needs feeding (half a scoopful of pony nuts) and exercise (halter in tack room). Then his stable needs mucking out. Tell my dad if you can't and he'll have to do it. But I know I can count on you.

From a suffering friend,

Penelope Potter

P.S. When you've finished, come straight to the house and tell me how Pebbles is.

that Ned's poster was magic? Did he know that the pony in the picture came alive, and that sometimes he might be actual pony size and sometimes as tiny as Percy, the smallest of her china horses? Annie was sure that no other pony poster in the whole world was so special or such a secret. She smoothed out the letter and cleared her throat.

"Oh, yes," cried Annie, flinging her window wide. By leaning out she could just see into Penelope's little stable yard. There was Pebbles, head out over his stable door, waiting for his breakfast. "I must go at once. See you later, Ned."

Then, not bothering to close the window, Annie raced for the door. The pony in the poster turned ever so slightly to watch her go.

Downstairs, Annie burst into the living room.

"I'm going to look after Pebbles," she informed everyone.

"I knew she would," said Jamie.

"Not before breakfast," said Dad, lifting the plate with all the toaster parts and putting it on top of the television.

"There is no breakfast," said Annie. "I burned it."

"And I've made some more," called Mom from the kitchen. "Toast is on its way. Put on your boots if you're going to muck out. I don't want manure all over your sneakers. You can take your toast with you if you're in such a rush."

"Thanks, Mom," said Annie, running into the kitchen to find her boots.

"What do you want on it?"

"Honey, please." Annie pulled off her sneakers and crammed her feet into her rubber boots. She took the offered toast.

"Here," said Mom. "You can give Pebbles these with my compliments." And she handed Annie a paper bag. Annie shook it. "Carrot sticks," explained Mom. "Nice long ones so he won't choke. You can add them to his pony nuts. And give Penelope my love when you go and see her. Tell her I hope she gets better soon."

"I will," said Annie and, with the toast between her teeth, she flung open the back door, hurried across the grass, and around the house to the side gate.

Once on the road, Annie set off purposefully toward Penelope's stable. This was the first time she had ever looked after Pebbles all by herself and she was really excited. It made up for her disappointment that Ned's magic was not working today. She chewed her toast, hardly noticing that she was eating. By the time she reached the stable yard gate, there was only the crust left. She held it between her teeth while she undid the latch.

A long, low whicker came from Pebbles's stable.

"I know, I know. You're saying, 'where's my breakfast?'" Annie held out her hand, fingers flat, balancing the toast crust. Pebbles's lips wobbled open and the crust was gone. He crunched happily while Annie stroked his dappled gray neck and looked in the stable. "Not a wisp of hay left. No wonder you're hungry." Smelling the carrots, Pebbles pushed at the paper bag. "No! You can have the carrots with your breakfast. I'll get it now."

Annie ran to the tack room and opened the door. She was greeted by the inviting smell of leather, saddle soap, and pony. Lifting the lid of the feed bin, she measured half a scoopful of pony nuts into a bucket and shook the carrot sticks on top.

As Annie left the tack room, another long, low whicker greeted her, and Pebbles, with ears pricked, stretched his neck toward his breakfast. Annie held the bucket behind her as she undid the stable door.

"Back, Pebbles," she commanded and the pony stepped politely out of the way. But the moment she put down the bucket, his head was in it. Annie shut the door and smiled. "Breakfast at last, eh boy?"

"Yoo-hoo, Annie!"

Annie turned to find Mrs. Plumley, their neighbor from next door, beaming at her from the gate, and Ruddles, Mrs. Plumley's dog, wagging his tail.

"Hello, Mrs. Plumley," said Annie, skipping over. "Hello, Ruddles." Annie bent down as the little dog pulled against his leash to say hello. She gave him a big cuddle and Ruddles gave her a big lick. "Oh, help," she cried. "Right on the nose."

"He doesn't mind noses, Annie." Mrs. Plumley chuckled. "He gives all his friends big doggy kisses, don't you Ruddles?"

"*Woof, woof,*" barked Ruddles in agreement.

"Now where's young Penelope this morning? Her mom told me she was off to a horse show today."

"She's not feeling very well," said Annie. "So I'm looking after Pebbles."

There's Magic in Every Book!

The Rainbow Fairies
Books #1–7

The Weather Fairies
Books #1–7

The Jewel Fairies
Books #1–7

The Pet Fairies
Books #1–7

The Fun Day Fai
Books #

SCHOLAST

www.scholastic
www.rainbowmagi

How can one Pet cause so much Trouble?

Runaway Retriever

Loudest Beagle on the Block

Mud-Puddle Poodle

Bulldog Won't Budge

Oh No, Newf!

Smarty-Pants Sheltie

Dachshund Disaster

...s and find out! ....